THE DEMOCRATIC
IDEAL IN EDUCATION

MAXWELL PRESS

THE DEMOCRATIC
IDEAL IN EDUCATION

R. E. HUGHES

Author of "Schools at Home and Abroad,"
"The Making of Citizens: A Study in
Comparative Education, etc.

MAXWELL PRESS

Chennai   New Delhi

MAXWELL PRESS

An Imprint of MJP Publishers

ISBN 978-93-5528-187-6   MAXWELL PRESS

No. 44, Nallathambi Street,
Triplicane,
Chennai 600 005

MJP 1415   © Publishers, 2022

Publisher : **C. Janarthanan**

PUBLISHER'S NOTE

The legacy of a country is in its varied cultural heritage, historical literature, developments in the field of economy and science. The top nations in the world are competing in the field of science, economy and literature. This vast legacy has to be conserved and documented so that it can be bestowed to the future generation. The knowledge of this legacy is slowly getting perished in the present generation due to lack of documentation.

Keeping this in mind, the concern with retrospective acquiring of rare books has been accented recently by the burgeoning reprint industry. MAXWELL PRESS is gratified to retrieve the rare collections with a view to bring back those books that were landmarks in their time.

In this effort, a series of rare books would be republished under the banner, "MAXWELL PRESS". The books in the reprint series have been carefully selected for their contemporary usefulness as well as their historical importance within the intellectual. We reconstruct the book with slight enhancements made for better presentation, without affecting the contents of the original edition.

Most of the works selected for republishing covers a huge range of subjects, from history to anthropology. We believe this reprint edition will be a service to the numerous researchers and practitioners active in this fascinating field. We allow readers to experience the wonder of peering into a scholarly work of the highest order and seminal significance.

MAXWELL PRESS

CONTENTS.

INTRODUCTION.

In our land there is to-day considerable discussion upon educational matters. Appeals are made sometimes to our reason, and sometimes to our prejudices, and considerable bitterness of feeling is aroused and displayed, and generally much pother is created upon matters that are only incidentally educational. Let us trust that out of this evil good may come. Let us hope that what is at present an interest produced artificially, and with much labour, may become perennial and natural. Let us seize this golden opportunity to make our people permanently interested in this fateful problem of national education, so that the popular apathy, which in the past has been our curse, may develop into a popular vigilance, without which no truly national system is possible. But popular vigilance needs popular intelligence. Until our people can be made to see the true inwardness of their own instinctive faith, until they can be made to realise what national training means, and to understand why we need a better system of education—not, indeed, to beat the German, but to beat the devil—only when these matters have become part of our common faith may we look for the regeneration of this land.

The superficial is always evident, but the spirit is rarely recognised. The splendid instructional efficiency of certain foreign systems of education easily seduces the casual observer, and sometimes even attracts the admiration of the uncritical philosopher. It is because I have felt that this unreasoning admiration of some of our people (some indeed of the best friends of education) for foreign systems of schools is a most serious danger to our own schools that I have written this essay. I hope that in it I have shown that, although we may learn much, we dare copy but little from the foreign schools. We must work out our own salvation. We must dare to be ourselves. We must realise that the school is deliberately designed to manufacture citizens of a certain peculiar, unique, and characteristic type. Our schools and teachers must be content to turn out English children, and leave the turning out of German children for the German school. I have endeavoured to bring out the contrast between the social ideals of different peoples in this essay, and to show how in these matters of national education we must be content to look westward, not eastward, for light.

I have to thank my friend Mr. P. B. Balland for kindly reading the proofs for me.

R. E. HUGHES.

Christmas, 1903.

CHAPTER I.

National Types and Educational Ideals.

" . . . during the civilisation period, the body being systematically wrapped in clothes, the *head* alone represents man—the little mannikin, intellectual, self-conscious man, in contradistinction to the cosmical man represented by the entirety of the bodily organs."—E. CARPENTER.

As my purpose here is to endeavour to describe a movement in education which has become international in character, and to show how this democratic ideal of peoples is being materialised in the various national systems of education, it will be necessary for us to give some attention to the present aspect of the social organisms in those countries; for the educational system of any country is based upon, and reflects clearly, the many political and social factors that go to the making of the national life.

A system of education is so far national and peculiar only so far as it vividly and accurately reflects the many ripples that constitute the stream of a people's life. You will best realise the characteristics, and, indeed, the ideals, of a people only by carefully investigating the working of its schools. Go among the children in its schools if you would find the pole star of a nation's hopes. And so just as there is complexity in the social organism so is there complexity in the system of schools; and just as it is difficult to speak of a unity in the national life, so is it difficult, if not impossible, to speak of a unity in the national system of education. The social life of a modern people is infinitely complex; so, too, is their system of education. The school reflects this diversity in unity of a people. And just as national characteristics are slowly disappearing, so, too, are educational differences. Yet, allowing this much, let us not lose sight of the enormous significance and power to-day of national characteristics and of national ideals. Beneath the apparent diversity and complexity of national life there is a great permanent fund of thought, action, and ideals that remains untouched by time and uninfluenced by environment. It is this great backwater of national characteristics that adds diversity to the picture of social progress to-day. We see the same force acting upon different peoples with very different results; and the only term that is common to the social unrest of to-day is its universality.

There can be small hesitation in ascribing to the mechanical inventions of the last century and the consequent profound changes in man's environment, the social unrest of to-day. Men find themselves in a world which neither training nor tradition has prepared them for. The world has suddenly become filled with phenomena that experience has not expected. It is felt that our old methods, our old faiths, help us not at all in meeting successfully the problems of to-day. The past has been lost and the future not found. The terrible growth of great cities, with their appalling poverty, the exacting cruelty of modern commercialism, the tyranny of capital, which laughs at loyalty and patriotism while exploiting them for its own ends, the seizing of public wealth for private ends, the puerility of politics, the bankruptcy of religion, and the annual holocaust of childhood on the altar of industrialism,—all these things are troubling the minds of philosophers and filling the hearts of the thoughtful with anguish. These problems are international : they are no nation's monopoly. In France and Germany they are as striking as in England and America. To find a paradise for children one must search mid the snows of Greenland or the forests of equatorial Africa. The ample folds of " Old Glory " cannot hide the child from the sweater,* and to-day there are probably more

---

* Here are two recent cuttings :—" The Italian Consul at Philadelphia, Count Brandolini, aroused by the exposures of the *New York Journal*, recently made a thorough investigation of the labour conditions in

child slaves under our Union Jack than under any other flag in the world.†

New Jersey, especially as they related to the children of Italians.   The Count said :—

"'I found men, women, and children living in absolute slavery. In the glass works of the George Jones Company I found thirty or forty children not more than eight or ten years old working under the most shocking conditions.   When I sought out their parents, I was met with the argument that unless the children worked as soon as they could earn anything they could not make a living.   They said they must all work or else starve.   The owners of the glass works contended that the children they employed were all above the legal age, but I know better.   Some of them looked to be little more than mere babies.'"

" Hundreds of small boys work for Mr. Borden, and many of them toil ten hours a day without a thread of clothing on their bodies.   A *Journal* man has investigated the matter and found that naked people work in the American works, but they are not exactly babies.   They are children, sometimes not more than fourteen years old.   They work in big tanks called 'lime keer,' in the bleach house, packing the cloth into the vats.   This lime keer holds 750 pieces of cloth, and it requires one hour and twenty minutes to fill it.   During that time the lad must work inside, while his body is being soaked with whatever there is of chemicals which enter into the process of bleaching, of which lime is a prominent factor.   The naked bodies of the children who do this work day after day are never dry, and the same chemicals which effect the bleaching process of the gray cloth naturally bleach the skin of the operator, and after coming out of the vats the boys show the effects in the whiteness of their skins, which rivals the cotton cloth."

† " Nor is this state of things confined to the Metropolis.   In Massachusetts the statistician of the labour bureau declares that among wage labourers the earnings (exclusive of the earnings of minors) are less than the cost of living ; that in the majority of cases working men do not support their families on their individual earnings alone, and that fathers are forced to depend upon their children for from one-quarter to one-third of the family earnings, children under fifteen supplying from one-eighth to one-sixth of the total earnings.   Miss Emma E. Brown has shown how parents are forced to evade the law prohibiting the employment of young children, and in Pennsylvania, where a similar law has been passed, I read how, forced by the same necessity, the operatives of a mill have resolved to boycott a shopkeeper whose relative had informed that children under thirteen were employed.   While in Canada, last winter, it was shown that children under thirteen were kept at work in the mills from six in the evening to six in the morning, a man on duty with a strap to keep them awake." —*Social Problems*, p. 91, H. GEORGE.

f C.

The truth is, indeed, that the mechanical inventions of the last century gave capital a lever that the State should have controlled.

So momentous is the responsibility of controlling this lever that for common safety it should be borne by all. It is a vague, instinctive feeling, that the lever is governed by the wrong hands, that is at the bottom of much of the social dissatisfaction of to-day.

Other suggestions have been thrown out, and innumerable have been the remedies suggested for the disease. Education, it was said, would prove the panacea of social evils. Build schools and you will close prisons, we were told. Time has, however, proved how delusive that dream was. Juvenile offenders, instead of diminishing as a result of building schools, have of late years enormously increased in every educated community. There has been, indeed, a softening of public opinion, and a consequent decrease in the number of prisoners, but the annual number of actual delinquents has, as I have said, not only at home, but in France, Germany, and most of all in America, gone on increasing to an appalling extent.

Education can never save a State whose foundation is based upon a false system of social economics. In Germany the best educated people in the world may be observed suffering from the same social ills as the people of America and England. Education alone can never regenerate a race. The happiness of a State is dependent upon the social well-being of its individual citizens, and to a man destined to perpetual social slavery education becomes a curse, not a blessing.

To educate a slave is the pastime of a tyrant. While the social organisation of society is such that the majority of thinking beings have nothing to think of but how to live, it is positive cruelty to place in their hands intellectual weapons, with which they may carve beautiful statuary it is true, but it crumbles to dust even in the very making. Let us free men from the thraldom of Nature, and of their fellows, before we urge them towards true freedom and real intellectual development. Poverty and tyranny will hide the stars from even the brightest of eyes and the most beautiful of souls. "Poverty is the Slough of Despond which Bunyan saw in his dream, and into which good books may be tossed for ever without result. To make people industrious, prudent, skilful, and intelligent they must be relieved from want. If you would have the slave show the virtues of the freeman, you must first make him free." ("Progress and Poverty," p. 219.)

The more potent causes of this universal social unrest are difficult to define correctly; nevertheless, that it is intimately connected with the problem of the ownership and distribution of the land is evident. In America, England, and Germany, and generally speaking, too, in the urban rather than in the rural area, are its effects most pronounced. In France, Switzerland, and Holland, for example, the minute sub-division of the land has undoubtedly minimised the evil, an evil which in its extreme form is seen in the enormous aggregations of capital known as Trusts, Combines, and Syndicates—social phenomena— which are undoubtedly leading even easy-going citizens to see the reasonableness and the practical effectiveness of State Socialism.

But it is not my purpose here to enquire into the many immediate causes of this social unrest, an unrest which, cosmopolitan as it is, shows how deep-lying and wide-spreading are its causes. More pertinent here is the investigation as to the relative efficiency, from a national point of view, of the various systems of education as reflecting the social organism itself.

A criterion of immense value here is the relative facility which a system offers for the growth of individuality, or, in other words, the adaptability and elasticity of the system itself. By this I mean the facilities that the State offers for the development and nourishment of individuality in its citizens.

It is deeply important to recognize the relative value of bureaucratic organisation and of individualism to the State. Both have immense advantages and serious limitations; but in England to-day there is undoubtedly a tendency to emphasise the value of national organisation and to estimate the efficiency of a State by the collective rather than by the individual capacity of its citizens. Germany is held up to us for admiration as a State where every individual is fitted for his task in life by the State. This is, indeed, true, and one's first thought is undoubtedly admiration for this beautiful machine, which apparently works so smoothly, and in which one part is so like another as to fit in the general scheme of things without any friction. For certain purposes, and within certain limits, the machine does excellent work. But it is travesty to speak of freedom under such circumstances. Every child in Germany, from the age of six, is seized by the State and deliberately trained to fill a certain place in the national machine. Every school in Germany is deliberately designed for turning out certain specific parts for this machine. Of course, occasionally, even in Germany, Nature refuses to conform, and we hear of boys and men who have been robust enough to break the shell that would bind them to their little part in the national life. "Under any condition of things," remarks Henry George in his *Social Problems*, "short of a rigid system of hereditary caste, there will, of course, always be men who, by force of great abilities and happy accidents, win their way from poverty to wealth, and from low to high position." But such are the exceptions, and even to-day it is easier for a man of intellect to achieve high position in China than in Europe.

Although, indeed, much is gained by this social co-operation, much, too, is lost. Under present conditions, with bureaucracy triumphant, Germany is bound in time to become a howling wilderness of intellectual mediocrity. Infinitely more valuable intellectually, and, in the end, commercially, too, is the supply of individuality which this system crushes. The national organisation which checks the flow of individual energy, or even endeavours to organise, control, and turn it into certain definite and clear channels, is bound to result in a considerable waste of national capital.

Not a few writers have seen in the national habit of Englishmen of working hard from their youth up, and so giving vent to a superfluity of animal spirits and energy, much of the secret of England's success. " In action," remarks Bagehot, " it is equally this quality in which the English—at least, so I claim it for them—excel all other nations. There is an infinite deal to be laid against us, and as we are unpopular with most others, and as we are always grumbling at ourselves, there is no want of people to see it. But, after all, in a certain sense, England is a success in the world ; her career has had many faults, but still it has been a fine and winning career upon the whole. And this on account of the exact possession of this particular quality. What is the making of a successful merchant ? That he has plenty of energy and does not go too far. And if you ask for a description of a great practical Englishman, you will be sure to have this, or something like it : ' Oh, he has plenty of go in him, but he knows when to pull up!' He may have all other defects in him, he may be coarse, he may be illiterate, he may be stupid to talk to; still, this great union of spur and bridle, of energy and moderation, will remain to him." (*Physics and Politics*, p. 202.)

National efficiency is too expensive when bought at the price of individual liberty. Bureaucracy is efficient but expensive; it kills all variety, all spontaneity, all resource. It makes of man a human machine, and sets artificial limits to his development and action. Certain great commercial advantages undoubtedly result from this national organisation; but there are some things that commerce can offer no compensation for, and this truth can receive no more striking confirmation than the contrast between the Germany of 1870 and that of 1900.

In Germany, and, to a lesser extent, perhaps, in France, the ideal of citizenship is this social one ; and we find the educational systems deliberately contrived to fit every child for his place in the State machine. In other lands, on the contrary, the rights of the individual to full development as a moral and intellectual being are placed as the first principle of school training, for in these lands the social ideal is not a communal but a personal one. Consequently, in these latter States, the aim and purpose of education is very much wider and has much less direct effect on the commercial organisation of the State than in the former States. To an American or to an Englishman education means much more than merely preparing the youth to take his place in the national industrial machine. It means, indeed, all those social factors that go to build up a liberal citizen and to make of the youth a ruler, not a producer. Such a community places character first; but this subordination of intellect to character should result in a recognition that the complete character is built upon the trained intellect. English people have instinctively recognised the better part of this truth, but not all of it, and in their admiration of character have rather lost sight of the indispensableness of intellect. However, national education in the Anglo-Saxon communities is a much more complex matter than it is in Continental communities, where a specific and definite purpose is ever present before the school. Hence in any comparison of national systems of education it is essential that these social ideals of peoples be recognised.

There are among the leading nations of to-day, as we have suggested, two ideals of citizenship, which these schools, as institutions deliberately designed for the propagation of national ideals, are endeavouring to materialise—one in which each individual is being trained to take his destined place in the national machine, and in which, consequently, the rights of the individual are subordinate to those of the community; and the other, in which the rights of the individual are recognised as supreme, and in which every facility is offered by the community for the full development of those gifts with which he has been blessed.

But, further, in any real comparison must be recognised the special aptitudes of different peoples. There is as great diversity among peoples as among individuals, and while some nations are naturally disposed to action, others are equally disposed to thought; some peoples are distinguished by a logical consistency in their actions, others are equally characterised by a kind of instinctive inconsistency; some nations flourish on compromise, others sacrifice themselves on the altar of symmetry and order.

The people of one race think first and act afterwards, those of another act first and think afterwards.

Hence we must recognise that in so far as the school is an intellectual force, it lends itself to the varying purposes and aptitudes of different peoples to a very different degree. Where a people have placed as their national ideal intellectual efficiency there will the scope and the power of the work of the school in the national life be greatest. The national ideal being an intellectual one, the work of the school, consisting as it essentially does of the propagation of national ideals, will be much simplified, and the effect of the instructional side of the school work will be great and marked on the national life itself. It is much easier work for the school to have as its one aim an intellectual rather than a moral ideal. Not that any people, or, indeed, any school, does or can altogether separate these two aims, but rather there is a subordination of the one to the other, according as the one or the other ideal looms the larger in the national horizon. When the moral ideal is supreme the work of the school becomes more complex, and, on the other hand, its influence as a political engine for the manufacture of citizens diminishes. So diverse is the nature of this moral ideal that the forces employed in its materialisation are of the most subtle and varied character. The school becomes then but one—an important one, it is true—among the numerous influences that go to the building up of this moral ideal. The work of the school, though important, is not indispensable, and its effects lack the directness and solidarity that characterise the work of a school whose first aim is intellect. Hence there is a certain vagueness, a want of directness, a lack of intellectual grip, an amateurishness, about the work of the school that give rise to considerable criticism and to some distrust, especially among the more intellectual elements of the community.

But further than all this, is there not amongst our people to-day as dangerous a tendency to deify intellect and to exaggerate the value of knowledge to a people? This fact, that knowledge has an extrinsic and utilitarian value, is a most dangerous weapon to use for argument, for its logical outcome is the destruction of all liberal education. So far, indeed, has this policy proceeded in some countries, that in their schools no really liberal training is given. The education provided is an *ad hoc* training, and is deliberately intended to fit the child for the immediate purposes of commercial, industrial or professional life. But education is in truth a much deeper matter than that. " Intellectual power and knowledge then, as guiding principles, are usurpers, and do not lead to perfection. . . . True education is nothing less than bringing everything that men have learnt from God, or from experience, to bear first upon the moral and spiritual being by means of a well-governed society and healthy discipline, so that it should love and hate aright, and through this, secondly, making the body and intellect perfect, as instruments necessary for carrying on the work of earthly progress, training the character, the intellect, the body, each through the means adapted to each."—(Thring : *Education and School*, p. 22.)

In the democratic State, where each child must be trained, firstly, to be a citizen and only subsequently a craftsman, and where the obligation of the community to provide all means for self-development is recognised, such a subordination of the individual to the communal rights as I have described above would be utterly repugnant.

In such a community as England the first purpose of school training is the making of citizens, the rearing of men and women prepared for the duties of government. Hence in such a country's schools the science of politics, the duties of citizenship, should occupy a prominent position in the curricula.*

---

* " To live in such a city was in itself no mean training for a man, though he might not be conscious of it. The great object of Pericles' policy had been to make Athens the acknowledged intellectual capital and centre of Greece, 'the Prytaneum of all Greek wisdom.' Socrates himself speaks with pride in the Apology of her renown for ' wisdom and power of mind.' And Athens gave her citizens another kind of training also through her political institutions. From having been the

For each child must needs be educated to take his part in the system of government, and as the value of any discussion or action depends not only upon the number, but also upon the variety and diversity of the forces at work, so it becomes clear that the searching for and fostering of individuality is of the highest importance and value to such a democratic community.

" Again, upon plausible grounds—," remarks Bagehot, "looking, for example, to the position of Locke and Newton in the sciences of the last century, and to that of Darwin in our own—it may be argued that there is some quality in English thought which makes them strike out as many, if not more, first-rate and original suggestions than nations of greater scientific culture and more diffused scientific interest.   In both cases I believe the causes of the English originality to be that government by discussion quickens

---

head of the confederacy of Delos, she had grown to be an Imperial, or, as her enemies called her, a tyrant city. She was the mistress of a great empire, ruled and administered by law. The Sovereign Power in the State was the Assembly, of which every citizen, not under disability, was a member, and at which attendance was by law compulsory. There was no representative government, no intervening responsibility of ministers. The Sovereign people in their Assembly directly administered the Athenian empire. Each individual citizen was thus brought every day into immediate contact with matters of Imperial importance. His political powers and responsibilities were very great. He was accustomed to hear questions of domestic administration, of legislation, of peace and war, of alliances, of foreign and colonial policy, keenly and ably argued on either side. He was accustomed to hear arguments on one side of a question attacked and dissected and answered by opponents with the greatest acuteness and pertinacity. He himself had to examine, weigh, and decide between rival arguments. The Athenian judicial system gave the same kind of training in another direction by its juries, on which every citizen was liable to be selected by lot to serve. The result was to create at Athens an extremely high level of general intelligence, such as cannot be looked for in a modern State." (F. J. CHURCH, *The Trial and Death of Socrates*—Introduction.)   Again : " Mr. Galton, however, has expressed the opinion, and most of those who have written on the social condition of Athens seem to agree with him, that the population of Athens, taken as a whole, was as superior to us as we are to Australian savages."—MR. SYMONDS, in his *Sketches in Italy and Greece ;* quoted by Lord Avebury in his *Pleasures of Life*, p. 186.

and enlivens thought all through society; that it makes people think no harm may come of thinking; that in England this force has long been operating, and so it has developed more of all kinds of people ready to use their mental energy in their own way, and not ready to use it in any other way, than a despotic government.   And so rare is great originality among mankind, and so great are its fruits, that this one benefit of free government probably outweighs what are, in many cases, its accessory evils.   Of itself it justifies, or goes far to justify, our saying with Montesquieu, ' Whatever be the cost of this glorious liberty, we must be content to pay it to Heaven.' "   (*Physics and Politics.*)

On the other hand, in the well-organised or bureaucratic State every child passes through the same mill and is turned out so like his mates as to be indistinguishable from them. He thinks in the same channels, believes in the same faiths, and has the same stolid indifference to all higher aspirations and ambitions: school has effectually crushed his individuality, and so minutely stratified and differentiated is the world in which he lives that even had he the will he has not the power to alter his environment and impinge his personality on his surroundings.

But in the democratic State the liberty of each personality is recognised.   The sacredness of the individual is admitted. Nothing matters before this—the right of each child to full development; to this everything must be sacrificed. He who hinders the growth of childhood into full complete manhood is guilty of high treason to the State. He who, by word or deed, attempts to curb the growth of children, either intellectually, morally or physically, by limitations of age or opportunity, is a deadly enemy to the commonwealth.   This right of childhood to complete development is the foundation stone upon which is built the temple of true democracy. Everything must be sacrificed to that.   Our system must be elastic and comprehensive; it must allow childhood to grow into citizenhood as free and as unfettered as the sunlight that kisses the curls of children. We must give up all for that liberty of spontaneous development.   National efficiency bought at the price of liberty is too dear. High intellectuality is worth much, but serene national morality is worth infinitely more. For, after all, let us beware of this idol of intellectuality. Education is not a mere accumulation, not a mere physical process, but a spiritual growth.

Intellect appeals to intellect as deep calls to deep. Let us, however, beware of these strange leaders who would entice us out into the barren wastes of intellectuality, where without our moral stamina and resource we should quickly die.

Nay, but let us hold fast to our old faiths, and be guided by our own instincts and aptitudes, which have in the past made us what we are, and which will, an we cling to them, never play us false in the future. Let us beware of placing this Teutonic god of intellectuality in our schools, but rather let us be true unto ourselves, unto our own ideals ; and whatever the future has in store we shall meet it as honest men, panoplied in the armour of our own integrity, and loyal to the truth that in us as a people lies.

CHAPTER II.

The Democratic Ideal in Education.

STANDING on the Rigi and looking eastward towards the rising sun, one's eyes pass over a panorama of exquisite beauty. At our feet, as it were, lies the little town of Schwyz, at the head of the Lowerzzee, nestling 'neath the frowning crags of the two Mythen, whilst stretching away towards the right and kissing the horizon like a silver arc, lie in one huge semicircle those giants of Central Europe— the Bernese Alps.

Here and there tiny ribbons of silver twist in and out the green background of the picture, showing where the boisterous Reuss or rushing Aar pursue their tumultuous courses. Far in front of us, almost lost in the haze of the horizon, peep the Tyrolean Alps ; and between them and us many are the gaps and ravines that Nature has left unfilled. She has protected this little land of Switzerland with wondrous solitude and care,* as if to serve for the growth and protection of one of her most beautiful flowers ; but here towards this Austrian land her fortress is left vulnerable, and many have been the bitter battles that her carelessness have caused. It is nearly six hundred years ago since there on that meadow beneath us took place such a fight as the world rarely sees. It was on that field of Morgarten that the poor peasantry of Switzerland hurled

---

* "The great, wealthy, and powerful nations have always lost their freedom ; it is only in small, poor, and isolated communities that liberty has been maintained."—*Social Problems*, p. 16 (H. George).

back the feudal chivalry of Austria.   Armed with but their own poor weapons and stout hearts these sons of Swiss soil showed the proud barons of Germany that, though men may decree distinctions of rank, God dissolves them in the moment of battle, and that on the touchstone of life your prince and your peasant are very equal indeed.

And so it was here mid Alpine snows that true democracy first saw the light.*   It was for many a year afterwards a very tender child: slowly it grew and gradually.   In Europe, indeed, excepting in the bracing atmosphere of mountainous countries, it has rarely thrived.   In Norway, Scotland, and Wales it has grown steadily, but slowly.   In America, however, it has reached the full stature of manhood, and the great gulf stream of ideas that animates and sustains this world of ours is now rushing in full force across the Atlantic from America to Wales, Scotland, and Norway, and so onward to Europe.

But now let us examine, with somewhat more detail, what are the ideals of democracy which, it is everywhere admitted, are such potent forces in modern societies.

It may be urged that all modern and civilised States, such as England, France, Germany, and the United States (to name the more important ones) are in truth democratic, and yet look at the extraordinary diversity of their social life and ideals !   How is it possible to find any common principle animating these four organisms ?   In America and, to a less extent, in England the ideals of true democracy are, it may be admitted, slowly materialising themselves ; in France, and still less in Germany, the only equality is that of the polling booth, and the utter futility of that as a basis for true democracy was long ago scoffed at by Carlyle.

---

* " Ye crags and peaks, I'm with you once again !
   I hold to you the lands you first beheld,
   To show they still are free.   Methinks I hear
   A spirit in your echoes answer me,
   And bid your tenant welcome to his home
   Again.   O, sacred forms, how proud you look,
   How high you lift your heads into the sky !
   How huge you are : how mighty and how free ! "

In France there is a legal equality of manhood; but the French people may be regarded as a pyramid of officials, which begins and rests upon the peasantry and workmen, and, passing through a hierarchy of public functionaries, culminates in the President. In Germany the same holds true, excepting that the Emperor is the apex of the pyramid.

In America there is no pyramid, the President is simply a shooting star—a meteor that is for a moment bright against the dead uniformity of the azure blue, only to sink again to the normal level of citizenship when his task is o'er. In America there is no official class: everyone may be an official to-day and to-morrow, but he is always a citizen. In Germany and France, on the other hand—once an official always an official—and it is only by accident that one is a citizen. This is a most important distinction to note between the ideals implied or understood of modern States, and to English people it is indispensable that this distinction should be recognised and properly appraised.

We are, by our geographical position, the half-way house between Europe and America, and in our social and educational ideals we are subject constantly to the attraction of these two very different ideals. Let me endeavour to bring out concisely these two ideals, more particularly as exemplified in the educational machinery of these States. In Europe every individual is looked upon as part of the State machine; and whether it be as soldier, teacher, or merchant, he is deliberately trained by the State for that purpose. The only "rights" of the individual in such States is his right to be perfectly trained to take his preordained place in the national machine. Consequently, in such communities each school has a definite and clear task set it; every school in such a State provides an *ad hoc* education for its pupils. A liberal education as understood in America or England is unknown in such a country.

In the true democratic State, on the contrary, such as America, the right of each individual is recognised as paramount. The foundation-stone of such society is that every member of the community is entitled to full development. It is held that it is the first duty of the State to fit all its children for full complete citizenship, *firstly for the sake of the child and only secondly for the sake of the State.*

In such a State it is held to be a wicked heresy to deny any child of the State full opportunities for training. Not only must the precocious child be allowed full growth, but every child. To place artificial limits either of age or of class is to be false to the teaching of true democracy and to be disloyal to the State. Nay, more, it is better for the State to waste somewhat of its resources in finding its intellectual treasures than to risk losing them altogether. For in such a State neither the tonnage of its merchantmen nor the price of its consols counts against the children in its schools. It is there in its schools that its national capital is banked.*

It is unnecessary to point out how in these matters we English people, with our natural tendency to compromise, seem to have hit the happy, or, perhaps, unhappy mean, and, as a people, we are subject constantly to these opposing forces, as represented by the bureaucratic systems of Europe and the free, unprofessional system of America.†

---

* " For greatest of all the enormous wastes which the present constitution of society involves is that of mental power. How infinitesimal are the forces that concur to the advance of civilisation as compared to the forces that lie latent ! How few are the thinkers, the discoverers, the inventors, the organisers, as compared with the great mass of the people ! Yet such men are born in plenty ; it is the conditions that permit so few to develop."—*Progress and Poverty*, p. 332.

† It is difficult to summarise this matter concisely, but it may be put thus : In the European State the future of the individual is irrevocably settled at an early age, and it is practically impossible for him to reverse this decision. But it is a matter of daily experience that the real aptitudes of individuals are often developed comparatively late in life. Now, in such a democratic State as America, no unnecessary obstacle is placed in the way of the individual cultivating these special aptitudes, even though they may appear late in life. Hence the career of a democratic American appears to the European curiously diversified and unprofessional. How can a man be a judge to-day and president of a University to-morrow ? To me this ready adaptability of the social organism is of immense value to the State ; but, on the other hand, there can be no doubt but that it lends itself to a good deal of charlatanism, and encourages superficiality and smartness at the expense of thoroughness.

C

Fortunately for our serenity, we, as a people, are really not very much interested in these educational matters—there are so many other momentous matters, such as football matches and horse racing, to engage our attention, that it is only when our religious leaders come out into the market place and beg us to save the State from that arch-fiend, the enemy, or when, again, some doleful spirit assures us that our commercial supremacy is going or gone because Germany makes more aniline dies than we do, that we are at last stirred to take a spasmodic interest—not, of course, in education (that is really too much to expect), but in certain aspects of school work.

I have said that England is the half-way house: it is the battle-ground between two ideals—between two conceptions of social co-operation—between two views of life. Here meet two great streams of modern thought—the individualistic, in which the rights of the individual are admitted as supreme, and the socialistic, in which these individual rights are indeed recognised, but not as supreme —rather as subordinate to the State.   Hence in our public life to-day there are to be observed two great streams of thought.   The first, the socialistic, looks to Germany for its ideal.   It sees in the disciplined obedience, the magnificent organisation, the high standard of intellectual skill of the Fatherland, its ideal.

This party is characterised by its high standard of intellectuality—its respect for culture—its desire of instructional efficiency in the school, and is apt to imagine that by inscribing on its banner the magic word " efficiency " it has captured the Rosetta stone that will read the riddle of national success.   But are we not all for efficiency now-a-days ?   Let us beware lest we become the victims of a phrase.

The other stream of thought is too instinctive for utterance.   It is because it is so true that it is so silent. The great forces of the universe are so deep as to be noiseless ; the little ones so superficial as to be harsh, strident and grating.   So this deep instinctive thought of the English people—that which sees in the free, spontaneous development of each individual the highest good of the State, looks across the Atlantic for its ideal and sees in the crowned glory of the setting sun the crimson radiance of the dawn.

If we consider for a moment this question of individual liberty it will be observed that in the evolution of the ideal three phases are distinguishable. The development of freedom may be represented by three concentric circles. Thus the innermost and smallest circle will represent man and his environment under that phase of liberty which, to my mind, is best defined by the word *legality*. This is the first stage wrung from wrong by humanity, and in it the highest good of citizenship is the equality of all men before the law. The next, a larger circle, corresponding to a fuller environment of man, I would designate the era of *fraternity*, in which not only are the liberties greater, but so also are the corresponding obligations. In this stage in the evolution of society men are banded together as brothers of a family for mutual help and defence, and within the family or nation the mutual obligation of each to all and all to each is fully recognised as combined with a corresponding freedom. But, just as the family has a head man in the father, so such a community has for its head a King, Emperor, or President. Whatever be his title, he is *in loco parentis* to all the members of the community, and, just as in the organisation of families each individual is trained to undertake certain tasks and fill recognised and definite positions, so in such States every member is deliberately trained for certain duties and is allocated to predetermined positions.

But the outermost, widest circle of all represents the third phase in the development of human liberty, and this phase I designate as the era of *Equality*. Here the freedom of each individual member of the community is absolutely complete : not only is he free before the law, not only is he socially free within the community, but he is free in all— free to become whatever his Maker intended him to be. Every man in this phase of society has absolute equality of opportunity. Whether he be the son of a peer or of a ploughman, whether boy or girl, man or woman—nothing whatsoever may stand between the individual and complete development.* In such a State even a peer's son will be allowed to grow up a useful, cultured member of society ; he will not be expected to pass an empty, idle existence between Pall Mall and Piccadilly; and if a nobleman have genius, such a community will not think it its duty to banish him to the boisterous atmosphere of an Upper House, but will allow him to utilise his abilities in the manner most conducive to communal prosperity.

In Germany the duty of the individual to the community is recognised ; in America not only that, but also the obligations of the community to the individual are admitted. I look upon this practical equality of opportunity of the American Commonwealth as the ideal towards which we here in England must move. Of course, like all ideals, this has its limitations. If we would obtain it we must be prepared to sacrifice much that is dear to some English people. We must, for a time at any rate, tolerate a certain amount of inefficiency, a loss of practical effectiveness, a lack of economy in working, and generally a want of directness and completeness in administration.

I think that the reader will best understand what I mean if I say that the German and French systems of education are *tidy*, whilst those of England and America are *untidy*. The democratic systems, for a time at any rate, are characterised by a lack of definiteness and clear outline. The true democracy is neither afraid of the overlapping of different classes of schools, nor is it prepared to draw lines of demarcation between schools primary and secondary. This cry of over- lapping generally arises from class jealousies and from people who before all else want a *tidy* system, in which the sphere of operations of each school is clearly and rigidly laid down.

---

*" Bring horse and man to the water, let them drink it if and when they will ; the child who desires education will be bettered by it, the child who dislikes it only disgraced."—*Ruskin.*

The bureaucracy of such countries as France or Germany will for many years doubtless be able to turn out better instructed parts for the national machine. But let us not forget that our conception of education means much more than mere instruction. By it we connote all those factors, visible and invisible, that go to build up the individual character in accordance with the national ideal ; and that ideal has a deeply ethical and spiritual basis that cannot be analysed or evaluated.

Education in a true democracy is so complex a matter as to be beyond the work of any school, however efficient. Education is in truth self-knowledge, self-reverence, self-control. It is the drawing out (not the putting in) of each individual whatever is noblest and best in him. In a true democracy the divinity of the personality of each individual is recognised. In such a community it is recognised that there is within each child of the State some effulgence, as it were, of the Eternal. It is not the piling of facts in a child's head, but it is the developing outward from the child's heart of his reverence for the Good, the Beautiful, and the True. It is a liberating of the " imprisoned splendour " that is within us all. Every child has within it a spark of the Eternal, a flash of the Infinite, and it is the work of the school to make visible and real that spark and flash. Education—true education—is indeed a revelation in self-consciousness.

In the true democratic State the educational ideal is so to organise and complete the national school that there may be provided for each child of the State every means of full growth—mental, physical, and moral.

In such a school so elastic must be the curriculum and methods as to allow full freedom for individuality to develop. The curriculum must fit the child, not the child the curriculum. In such a State the idea of a curriculum drafted by a central authority, and intended for use in all schools, such as is the case in France and to a less extent in Germany, is utterly repugnant. Not only will each school have a curriculum peculiar and appropriate only to itself, but, having laid in the primary school the foundations of all culture, there will in the secondary school be found room for a curriculum peculiar and appropriate to each individual child. The sanctity of personality must be recognised if the school is to be a really national school. It is a wicked heresy which attempts in any way to crush or warp the growth of individuality in the school.

The schools of France and Germany and England are to-day busily transmuting the precious gold of individuality and personal variety into the gross and base brass of uniformity. The splendid school systems of France and Germany are, in this respect at any rate, the curse of child-hood, and I confess that to me there is an infinitely greater potency and value in the ignorance of an Elizabethan England than in the organised culture of a modern Europe.*

The conception of equality of opportunity for all—" all for each and each for all "—is the working hypothesis, so to speak, of the true democratic State. Let us now consider how this principle may be carried out in the State system of education, how it affects the administration, the curricula, and the methods of the school; for all these, be it remembered, are conditioned by the school's ideal and purpose.

The outstanding characteristic of a national system of education in the democratic State is, that as in such State there are no class distinctions, so in its schools the only distinctions recognised are those dependent upon variations in intellectual and moral capacity. Hence in this State there are no class schools, no sectarian schools, no undenominational schools; indeed, there are no primary schools, no secondary schools; in fine, in such a community but one school is found, and that is the *national school*. In such a system there is absolutely no class distinction between one school and another or one teacher and another. The secondary scholar and teacher will differ from the primary scholar and teacher only in so far as their intellectual equipment and task vary. In this national school every

---

* " It is taken for granted that any education must be good ; that the more of it we get the better ; that bad education only means little education ; and that the worst thing we have to fear is getting none. Alas, that is not at all so. Getting no education is by no means the worst thing that can happen to us."—RUSKIN.

child of the State will be found—those under twelve or fourteen in the lower school, and those above that age and with fuller intellectual abilities in the upper school.   The essential solidarity of the national system of schools is fully recognised , in the democratic State.   There is in such a community but one national school and teacher.

From the Kinder-Garten to the primary school will be the history of the school-life of every child of the State, and with that training over 90 per cent. of the State's children must needs be content; but the others—the future intellectual aristocracy, the social and political leaders of the people— those who already show, not by examination, but by their whole school life, as watched by the teacher, the possession of special ability and aptitude; these, I say, that are the only real national capital, will proceed to the national secondary school, where they will receive that further development and training which it is the blessed privilege of the community to provide for them.

These children will proceed to the secondary school not because of unusual precocity, as evidenced in a competitive examination, but because of unusual intelligence as evidenced in a school career.

But further than this solidarity of the national school must be recognised the right to mutual independence of each constituent section of that school, namely, the Kinder-Garten, and the so-called primary and secondary schools.   In the true democratic State these are mutually independent, none is recognised as subordinate or preparatory to the other.   They are equal and self-contained. The task of each is essentially identical, namely, to develop the child fully, freely and spontaneously during the years it is a pupil there.

Each school will consider no matter but this—how best to educate the child for full citizenship.*   And the national

----

* " He had been eight years at a public school, and had learnt, I understand, to make Latin verses of several sorts in the most admirable manner.   But I never heard that it had been anybody's business to find out what his natural bent was, or where his failings lay, or to adapt any kind of knowledge to *him.   He* had been adapted to the verses,

school has no other task but this—it is to give the State a constant supply of citizens, an army of well-trained privates and a corps of carefully selected and highly cultured officers, trained to citizenship, not to any form of craftsmanship. The national school must content itself with a liberal education. Specialisation in any form must follow, not accompany, this liberal training. I would emphasise this right to perfect independence not only of each constituent department of the national school, but of the school itself as a whole. This school must train for life. It must prepare its pupils for the aggregate common life, not the life of the counting-house or the consulting-room.

Further, any school that is looked upon merely as a preparatory school to another school must suffer. The Kinder-Garten undoubtedly suffers from being looked upon as preparatory to the primary school, and the primary suffers when considered as a feeder for the secondary, and the secondary school, in its turn, suffers when treated merely as a fitting school for the University. I am afraid I shall be misunderstood ; but, if you will consider the matter, you will see that what is needed is not a modifying of curricula from below upwards, as is now the case, but rather from the top downwards. The reform of curricula must begin in the University, not in the Kinder-Garten. In brief, I may state my point of view thus : When the independence of each school and its true duty towards the child have been recognised, then each department—

---

and had learnt the art of making them to such perfection that if he had remained at school until he was of age I suppose he could only have gone on making them over and over again unless he had enlarged his education by forgetting how to do it. Still, although I have no doubt that they were very beautiful, and very improving, and very sufficient for a great many purposes of life, and always remembered all through life, I did doubt whether Richard would not have profited by someone studying him a little instead of his studying them quite so much."— *Bleak House*, C. DICKENS.

However, this studying of childhood must not degenerate into the awful *analysing* of children as shown by Miss Blimber's treatment of poor little Paul Dombey. "It will naturally be very painful (to your father) to find that you are singular in your character and conduct."

primary, secondary, and academic—will receive the child completely (*i.e.*, harmoniously) developed, and will be prepared to continue that development a stage further. It will be for the primary school to build upon the foundation of the Kinder-Garten, for the secondary to build upon the work of the primary, and for the University to complete the edifice by building upon the work of the secondary school. Until this independence of the school is recognised it will suffer from diffusion of energy and be the victim of ignorant controversy.

It must be clearly recognised that the one purpose of all school training is the making of citizens—the building-up of men and women—cultured, loyal, resourceful—prepared for the burden and privileges of our civilization. Once this aim has been recognised there will be no longer heard these noisy, blatant cries for a commercial practical education. Of course, all true education must be practical. It must be built firmly on the rock of child experience and be knitted to the life the child will live, but to try and turn our schools into mere fitting-shops for the crafts is the very acme of a fatuous policy. The curriculum of every school must be real, then it will be practical. That is to say, the curriculum must be such as will make the child's own being (with its surrounding world) real and intelligible to him. His school training should make all that surrounds him real to him, and make himself intelligible to himself. Then will he know what duty, justice, reverence, truth mean ; he will understand that profound maxim of life, the golden rule ; and work will no longer mean the satisfying of the animal, but the fashioning of the spiritual within himself.

This criterion of reality in curricula brings out the futility of much of our present-day training. Our schools to-day, with their literary curricula, their constant appeals to the head, and their neglect of the heart or of the hand of the child, are offensive to the practical man, who feels in a vague, instinctive way that something is very wrong in a system of training which results in making country lads, town loafers, and labourers' sons, clerks. The fact is, indeed, that nothing is more patent than the unreality of our school training and the general detachment and aloofness of our school from the great world outside.

It is in the primary school that the seer will best cast the horoscope of a people. If there he sees mere intellect worshipped, instruction installed as god, and knowledge called power, then will the crystal become clouded, and the future dark with fateful possibilities ; if, again, he sees in a people's schools, and in a nation's high places, enthusiasm sneered at, knowledge despised, and earnestness scoffed at, then be sure that there, too, the prophet will see dark things in the glass, and his mind will be troubled with forebodings for the future. There is no feature of public life in England more heartrending than to observe the utterly false ideal of what is "good form" in society. In England alone is a professional man sneered at who takes his profession seriously. In England alone is it considered "bad form" for a man to talk "*shop*." Yet it is these men who talk "shop" and cannot say, or, perhaps, do "smart things," that are the salt of our people to-day, and they are the men to whom the nation instinctively turns in time of trouble. This desire for smartness and cleverness is the curse of our modern England.* The popular preacher, the successful politician is he who is continually saying and doing smart things. To be popular one must be cynical, pessimistic, and clever. The days when men in England believed in themselves, believed in their country and its civilising mission, have passed away.

To-day everyone, of course, believes in England's mission, but the point of view has altered. In the past this mission was sincerely and truly undertaken, because it *was* a

---

* " That will-o'-the-wisp hight, ' cleverness ' in schools and ' genius ' in more sapient regions, has sucked more into the filthy mantled pools of conceited ignorance or hopeless despair, and stopped more work than any other cause, besides being at the bottom of much false teaching, and luring nations to their destruction by false glitter. Prizes which few can win are dangled in the air by public opinion." And elsewhere the same writer observes :—" Cleverness is common enough, but the steadfast worth that can patiently endure is wanting."— *Education and School*, p. 35, THRING.

civilising mission; it was done for the sake of others; to-day it is undertaken for commercial purposes, and cynically admitted that it is done mainly for our own sakes. England to-day is suffering not from a poor school system so much as from two other immensely more important social forces. The first of these is the ideal of *amateurishness* that permeates the educated classes of England, and the second is the absolute indifference of the great mass of our people to all the nobler ideals of national life. If it were not for a few bright souls, who amid the gloom of indifference, cynicism, and ignorance that make up the national life, constantly keep alive the sacred flame of national culture, and with their hearts full of hope keep their gaze fixed upon the peaks and pinnacles, looking for the warm, red glow of the rising sun, I say if it were not for these few this England of ours would to-day be in a sad plight indeed. It is all very fine to speak of blazoning efficiency on your banner, but you must first engrave "earnestness" in the hearts of your intellectual leaders. England needs more character in her intellect even more than she needs more intellect in her character.

This worship of false gods—this veneration for superficiality, for mere smartness, for cleverness; in a word, this toleration of amateurishness throughout her national life must be abolished, must be relentlessly cut out, as a cancer, from the body politic, if England is to be worthy of and true to her mission. And having cut that out, the second curse of our national life will quickly disappear. This indifference to the higher ideals of life of the great mass of our people is largely due to the cynicism and hypocrisy of the intellectual leaders of the people. Get the guides and leaders out into the bracing and clear air of some mountain height, and they will see more reality and greater beauty, their vision will be clearer and wider, the tones of their voices will alter, the thoughts that move them to action will become deeper and broader ; and behold, when they beckon to their people and speak to them, more solemn will sound their voices, richer will be the imagination that prompts them, nobler and holier will be the ideals that animate them, and echoing down the heights will their thoughts pass until they find rest in the cottages below.

Let me now say a word as to the curriculum of this national school in the democratic State. The curriculum of any school is conditioned entirely by the purpose of the school. So that before we can proceed any further it is indispensable that we agree as to the purpose of the national school. Fortunately for us, that purpose is contained and implied in the title of the school. This school is deliberately designed by the State for the making of citizens.

That statement, however, though sufficient for ordinary purposes, is hardly embracing enough for us. We would go further, and say, " True, the State looks to its schools for its supply of citizens, but this term *citizens* is both vague and variable; cannot you tell us what you mean; what you aim at in this process of education; what is the really significant purpose of true education ?" and putting the matter thus we see we have at last touched bottom. What is the purpose of education ? Is it the acquisition of knowledge? Is it the training of the intellect? Is it the development of character ? Nay, it is none of these, but all of them. As Edward Thring once put it: " The whole system of schools in this country has been reconstructed at a vast expense, much of it permanent and unchangeable. What answer have these architects of mind given to the great question which their reconstructive work supposes them to have mastered ? Is education the making the mind full ? or is it making the mind strong ? Is teaching the putting in facts, or drawing out and practising latent powers ? Or is there something else not yet above the horizon ?" (*Theory and Practice*, p. 11.) And elsewhere he writes : " This transmission of life from the living, through the living, to the living, is the highest definition of education." (*Ibid*, p. 36.) Education is the fostering of power. All true education is a growth in power. Whatever makes the individual know himself better is education. For to know himself he must know and understand all outside himself, his environment of humanity and nature, and by so knowing clearly, intimately, and truthfully,* he will know what he is and what that is, he will see himself outside himself, he will project himself into the phenomena of the universe, he will recognise and so reverence the beautiful within himself, the true within himself, and the good within himself.   To know oneself is a complete education, for it means not only self-knowledge, but self-reverence, self-control ; and attaining those things we touch the ideal.

Hence, all education must be the development of the being ; anything that does not result in growth of power is not education. Knowledge that does not really enter into the fibre of the child's being is worse than useless ; it is only what is truly assimilated that is nutritious. And there is a limit, be it remembered, to the digestive capacities of children, even as there is to those of the City Fathers. I am convinced that in our schools to-day we are constantly forgetting this fact of the limitations of children's feeding powers. " Never try to fill the little mind with lumber under colour of its being of use by and by. Lumber does not excite thought, lumber does not interest, lumber does breed disgust ; nothing should be put into the mind which is not wanted immediately, and which is not also the easiest way of meeting the want." (THRING, p. 166.) Further, the unpalatable and nauseous nature of much of the food provided must not be forgotten ; yet despite these facts we thrust the food down wholesale, and then wonder that the children cannot retain it, but evacuate it at the first opportunity.

---

* " Training means accuracy. Observation and accuracy are twins. The beginning of all true work is accurate observation, the end and crown of all true work is an accuracy which observes everything, and lets nothing escape, a power of observation animated by a true love for what it undertakes to investigate, and able through love to discover subtler truth than other people. Observation and accuracy comprise all that it is possible for a teacher to do, whatever may be the subject with which he has to deal, and observation and accuracy ought first to be as the joy of the explorer to the curious child ; who should be made to see in every word he speaks, and every common thing he sets eyes on, endless surprises and novelties at every turn of unexpected pleasure and new delight."—THRING, *Education and School*, p. 102.

It is the fetish of knowledge that is enthroned as deity in our schools to-day.*   " Experience has shown that an undue attention to knowledge and undue honour paid to learning, is the characteristic of decline." (THRING, p. 123.) An old wag once said that *knowledge is power*, and the world has gone on repeating it ever since.

A much truer saying is that old Welsh maxim that the best weapon is the weapon of learning. It is not knowledge but the power of acquiring knowledge that is the real purpose of education. " Shoving in the regulation quantity into the pupils, to be pulled out again on demand, is one thing ; clearing the bewildered brain, and strengthening the mind, is another." (THRING, p. 133.)

The work of the school must be estimated by the amount of power that it develops in its pupils.† The power of doing, the power of thinking, the power of acquisition, the power of controlling and obeying, aye, and the power of believing, which is so sadly lacking in our schools of to-day, and which has resulted in that appalling lack of reverence

---

* " English schools have suffered from this fetish of knowledge to a greater extent, perhaps, than any other schools. Even to-day, to the vast majority of Englishmen, the success of a system of education is directly proportioned to the amount of knowledge of facts that a child carries away from school with him. We hear merchants complain that the boys coming into their offices from school are ignorant of book-keeping or shorthand, while the farmer complains that the school turns sturdy boys into weak and lazy labourers."

† " Every power of the child must be developed ; his spiritual, his intellectual, and his physical powers must each and all be trained to completeness if the school is to do its duty to the Nation. Not for the child's sake only—though this is an inalienable right of childhood—but for the community's sake must the pupil's powers be completely trained. I confess I find it difficult to understand how we can train the intellectual powers of childhood and ignore the spiritual and physical. The Nation needs complete children, not amputated *homunculi*. Let us train all our children, not portions of them. We must utilise the whole of our national capital ; for the powers of childhood are the gold mines of England. No Golconda yields riches so readily, so richly, and so luxuriantly as these. Let us, then, lay up for ourselves treasures here in this bank of a completely developed childhood."

for everything nobler than themselves in our children—it is these things that we must look for in our schools if we would have them give us good brave men and women, fully prepared for their tasks, and imbued with those deeper spiritual forces that are the wells whence the nation draws its life and strength. And may we not summarise the whole of this matter by saying that education is training. Education is not merely intellectual training—nor even only moral training—but it is indeed a training in self-control, which results from a full realising of self. To train the will is the great purpose of school life. It is not sufficient that one knows right from wrong : one must needs will the right and avoid the wrong. It is what one does, not what one knows, that matters. Habits, not facts, are what we must acquire.

Now let us consider how this power of which we have spoken may be developed in the school. Every child must be considered in three aspects, first as thinker, next as doer, and, thirdly, as worshipper : any system of education which neglects any one of these three aspects of human nature is incomplete and defective. Consequently, to develop the power of the child as thinker, actor and worshipper is the first purpose of school training ; but, further, it must be remembered that the child is not a mere point in space, absolutely indifferent to his surroundings. Nay, rather, his whole being will be constantly modified by his surroundings, and, indeed, this environment will be as much himself as he is. The world we live in is as much a real part of ourselves as we are, the personality of each one of us is like a coin with its obverse and reverse sides—they are different yet inseparable. Hence to know oneself is not merely to know ourself, but that other self, the outside self. To put it in another form, I would say that every child must be made intimately cognisant not only of itself, but of the civilisation and world into which it is born. And this world into which each of us is born and in which we move and live and have our being, is made up of two factors only—Nature and man. There is, on the one hand, that beautiful web of phenomena which Nature has spun around us, and, on the other hand, there are those many human souls that complete our world and round off our lives.*

So that school training must aim at developing the child as an actor, as a worshipper, and as a thinker—and to be an actor, thinker, worshipper, under right influences, he must know the world in which he lives. Therefore the purpose of any school whatsoever must be this growth of power in thinking, in doing, and in worshipping. Consequently, the curriculum of any school must contain those subjects only which fulfil this purpose.

To develop the child as thinker we must include the study of the mother tongue in, *e.g.*, *reading*, by which the thoughts of the race are made available to the pupil. By reading he is introduced to the master spirits of all time—to those men who have led and are leading us to the stars.† But, further, we must develop the child's power of thought expression by *speech*, *writing*, *drawing*, and the so-called *manual training*. To develop the child as actor we will include *history* in the curriculum. By history the child acquires the experience of the race, he learns his place in

---

* " Not knowledge, but the power of acquiring knowledge ; not the description of emotions, but the cultivation of right emotions ; not a being surfeited with facts culled from everywhere, but a being whose personality is in constant and exquisitely tuned responsiveness to all around it—that is the aim of all school training that is of real permanent national value."

† Reading is to the multitude what travelling is to the few By means of reading we extend the world of observation—it is like handing a telescope to the novice. Through it new worlds come into view. His life becomes at once more real—fuller and richer and wider. Nevertheless even into this new and wider world which books bring into his view the reader carries and projects his actual experience. What he reads of is painted on a canvas of his own making, what he sees in imagination is but his daily life of observation, writ larger or bolder it may be. And so it is that to appreciate fully the advantages of travelling, of beautiful pictures, of great books and noble ideals, one must needs be educated up to the standard of these books, pictures and ideals. Children are singularly irresponsive to beautiful scenery, and I know not a few admirable people whose recollections of Zermatt are inextricably mixed with *pâté de foie gras*, and those of Cologne with unpleasant odours.

society and his duties and privileges as citizen. It makes the world of to-day intelligible to him, and he becomes an actor under correct influences. To develop the child as worshipper of all that is good and true and beautiful, to develop within him that sense of reverence for nobler things, is the highest function of the school, and to do it we must call into play all those forces within our common life, whether they be religious, ethical or moral, that have lifted, and are lifting, our people to higher conceptions of duty and nobler ideals of conduct. To aid in this supreme work we will invoke the examples of history, the art of the musician, the painter, and the sculptor, and the sweet emotionalism and stern sense of duty of the poet and philosopher. We must teach our pupils the significance of the poet's words—

> I slept, and dreamed that life was beauty ;
> I woke, and found that life was duty.*

Lastly, we must consider the other—the environmental—side of the curriculum, the humanistic factor of which we have already met by our study of history ; but there is to be considered that world of Nature, organic and inorganic, that surrounds the child on every side, and which he must needs understand, if he is to be an actor, under the influence of complete knowledge and of right judgment.

Consequently, elementary physical science must needs form an indispensable subject in the curriculum of every

---

* " In the spiritual training we give him let it be our aim not to provide him with the data of certain forms of faith and ceremonial, but rather let us, with infinite endeavour, cultivate in him a correct attitude towards life. Nourish in him true reverence, foster in him real humility towards whatever is nobler and better than himself, and then for his faith the good God will provide. A right up-bringing means correct attitude, and this attitude is possible only when everything is reasonable. If we develop the whole of our child, and engender in him a many-sided interest in life, this will lead to a full knowledge, correct judgments, and a rational and reverential attitude toward all the physical and spiritual phenomena of the universe. We may, by formulæ and ordinances, produce in our children the similitude of reverence ; but true reverence, the reverence that lies at the base of a good man's character, can only be built upon understanding and knowledge."

school, and the science of number (*arithmetic*) is equally necessary, in order that the child may quantify and locate his experience.   The world of organic Nature will be made intelligible by the subjects of *Nature study* and *geography*. By a course in Nature study the child becomes acquainted with that teeming world of life around him, which is only equalled in its beauty by its diversity, and which develops in the child a reverence for Nature, a sense of responsibility towards himself, and a deep feeling of gratitude to his God. Finally, the child's knowledge of the world around him will be completed by a course in *geography* dealing with the surface features of the world in which he lives.

For complete education, then, I hold that this curriculum which we have sketched is, for essential purposes, the only curriculum available.   If the child of the State is to receive complete development, then all these powers must be developed in the primary school; whilst if special aptitude has been shown scholars will be sent on to the secondary school.

The curriculum of the secondary school should consist essentially of the same elements as the primary school.   It should be a fuller development of the primary school curriculum; thus the study of the mother tongue of the primary school will lead up to the fuller study of the mother tongue or other linguistic studies of the secondary school; the history of the homeland will lead up to the history of other lands in the secondary school, the sciences will become more exact, the geography will pass into physiography and the natural history sciences, whilst the arithmetic naturally leads to the mathematics of the secondary school.   Thus do we secure our solidarity of curriculum in the national school whether primary or secondary.   So you will observe that the main features of the democratic ideal in education are: The right of each child of the State to complete growth; the solidarity of the national school; the independence of each of its parts and of itself as a whole; the solidarity and unity of the curricula of the schools—the solidarity of the teaching profession; and, lastly, the recognition in the school of the sanctity of the personality of each child.

This may all appear very Utopian, idealistic and impossible to many ; nevertheless, I believe, with Emerson, in hitching my wagon to a star. It is by fixing our eyes on the stars and planting our feet on the earth that we shall at last reach the summit. And, after all, let us not forget that it is the aiming at, not the hitting of, ideals that is the motive force behind all human endeavour.

CHAPTER III.

The Ideal in Practice.

THERE is perhaps nothing more characteristic to-day of the modern world than the growth of the feeling of world citizenship. Against a certain type of patriotism the steam engine and electric telegraph have dealt a fatal blow—none the less fatal that its results are not clearly perceived. That ignorance is the greatest of curses, and that to it are due all misunderstandings and most quarrels, is to-day a truism. Distinctions of language will hinder this growth, it is true ; nevertheless, the careful observer to-day notes that beneath all the variety of national life, all the distinctions of national ideals, there are emerging certain aspects common to that life— to that ideal. He sees that there is a well characterised similarity amid the diversity of these national ideals, and that in all civilised communities to-day there is a remarkable sameness in the national aims and purposes, and that in the search for those aims and purposes are encountered the same obstacles. And first of all, and, indeed, chief of all, will he observe this struggle towards the democratic ideal in national life. Wherever he allows his eyes to rest he will observe the community agitated and troubled, almost as it were instinctively, by the desire of embodying this democratic ideal in the national life.

In Prussia the people's schools are completely controlled and partly maintained by the State. The government officials have complete control over curricula, and the teacher himself is a servant of the State.   Generally, too, the local managers themselves are government officials.   The local community, the people themselves, have no control or part in the management of the school; indeed, they are expressly forbidden from taking any active part in the education of their children, and the result is that there is little enthusiasm for education among the labouring classes.   The school is a denominational institution, each sect having a school for the use of its children.   So powerful, even to-day, are the two great sects, the Lutheran and the Catholic, of modern Germany, that their hold upon the schools, though not, indeed, so complete as in old days, is enormous.   In a certain narrow sense it may be affirmed that even to-day there are no purely State schools in Germany.   And although in Germany, as elsewhere, the everlasting struggle between State and Church has resulted in a certain loosening of the bonds of the Church upon the community, and that constant struggle has resulted in a certain enfranchisement of the schools from the control of the cleric, yet so powerful are the reactionary forces, and so united are these forces in this one endeavour, that constant compromise has been the rule, and only little by little has the freedom of the school been accomplished; and, as I have said, even to-day religion is the basis of the curriculum and the priest the arbiter of the fate of practically every school in Germany.   The growth of freedom of thought, and the development of social democracy have so far influenced but little the control of the primary school.   Nearly 70 per cent. of all Prussian primary schools are classed as Protestant schools, there are nearly 30 per cent. Catholic schools, and the remainder are Jewish schools and mixed schools, where the children of different sects are taught together in secular subjects, and separately in religious subjects.   In these primary schools over 90 per cent. of the children are educated.   In them are found children between six and fourteen years of age.   The regularity of attendance is remarkable, and is an admirable expression of the powers of Prussian bureaucratic organisa-tion.   The remarkable lowness of the figures of illiteracy in Germany generally is full proof of the effectiveness of this system of primary education as an instructional machine. There are, in fact, practically no illiterates in Germany to-day.

This system of Volksschulen "People's Schools," supported by the State and controlled by the Church and State, is primarily intended for, and, indeed, is utilised mainly by the labouring classes, which naturally constitute the great bulk of the nation. Only in a few spots and under somewhat unusual circumstances are these common schools used by classes other than the lower. They are to all intents and purposes class schools, and not common schools. The vast bulk of all other classes of the community have special schools for their children, where they are segregated and as clearly defined as cattle in an agricultural show. Germany is, in fact, still a country where the caste spirit is strongly felt, and where special schools for special classes of society are needed and supplied. There is indeed no true common school utilised by all classes of the community, and up to the present at any rate no special facilities have been provided for the passage of the clever pupil from one school to another. On the contrary, the future career of the German lad is effectually mapped out for him when his parent sends him it may be to the Volksschule or to the Vorschule of one or other type of secondary school at six or nine years of age. Although an attempt has been made of recent years to diminish the fatefulness of this choice, and in some cases to prolong the date of choice to the age of twelve, yet it is still true as a general statement of fact that there is in Germany no common school nor educational ladder; in other words, the democratic ideal is in Germany at present little more than a beautiful dream of educational and social reformers. Certain great intellects have, it is true, even in Germany forced a way for themselves from the primary through the secondary school to the university, but their triumph is but witness of the general failure. In Germany the intellectual treasures hidden amid the people are lost. They receive but the rough polish the common schools afford, so that they never sparkle as cut diamonds in the national crown.

So, too, is it in France. The State schools, both primary

and secondary, are controlled completely by officials, and the people themselves have practically no voice in the management of the schools. Officials at Paris frame the curricula for practically every school in France, and the details of organisation, appointment of teachers, selection of text books, etc., are entirely carried out by Government officials. The private Church schools are inspected as to certain matters by the Government officials, at whose will they may be opened or closed, but the actual administration of these schools is of course in the hands of the people who maintain them, that is to say, the congregations themselves. The vast bulk of the future citizens of France will be found in the Congregational schools or the State schools; but the *élite*, the odd five per cent. or so, will be found in the Communal College, the Lycée, or the Higher Conventual School. These latter will be as effectually cut off from the former as if Styx lay between.

The primary schools of France are intended for and utilised by the lower classes, and the secondary schools by other classes. There is no common school in France where the children of peasant and peer sit side by side, nor are the facilities for the passage of clever boys from one school to the other taken advantage of to any great extent. There is no common school and there is no educational ladder in France. There are, it is true, scholarships and bursaries provided by the State at the secondary school for the primary scholar, but the other expenses of the course are so great as to make it almost impossible for a poor man's son to accept them. This keen line of class distinction between primary and secondary school in France and Germany is also equally distinct between primary and secondary teacher. The solidarity of the profession, of which I have already spoken, is unknown in France and Germany; indeed so long as militarism—that Old Man of the Sea—maintains its present supremacy in Europe one cannot hope for any real democratic developments.

In England there is no democratic system of national education; indeed, strictly speaking, there is no national system of education in England to-day. There is a fairly comprehensive system of schools for the children of certain classes of society between the ages of three and fourteen, but these schools are not utilised by the middle and upper classes, and they bear no direct relationship to any schools that may exist above them other than the so-called higher elementary schools, which themselves are, to a large extent, class schools, and often appeal to a different section of the community from that reached by the average primary school. This English system of primary schools appeals only to and satisfies the needs of the majority of the community, but a majority made up of the lower classes, socially and intellectually. They have no direct connection with the secondary school, and the number of pupils who annually pass from the primary to any kind of secondary school in England is extremely small, if not, indeed, altogether negligible. It is probably smaller than even the very small number who do so in Germany, and much less probably than in France. In France, and, to a certain extent, in Germany, facilities are offered by the authorities for clever pupils to pass, by means of scholarships and bursaries, from the primary to the secondary school. In England this system is in existence only in the wealthier and more progressive communities. This lack of co-ordination between the primary and secondary school system of England is one of the most serious obstacles at present existing to the formation of a national democratic system of education in England, and it is an obstacle which cannot be surmounted for some time, at any rate ; for, truth to tell, there is at present no comprehensive system of secondary education in England to-day.

Of all the great modern commonwealths England stands in splendid isolation in her lack of appreciation of the absolute necessity for national well-being of a popular system of secondary education. The present fortuitous concatenation of teaching centres that passes for the English secondary system has within it some of the best, and many of the worst, schools in the world. The best are sometimes petrified by classicism, and the worst are always saturated by charlatanism.

The English public schools are, in some respects, unequalled elsewhere, for they have always placed character before intellect, and have inculcated ideals of conduct and discipline that in many respects are among the most valuable assets in public life.

Educators are constantly holding up for our admiration the primary school system of Germany, and insinuating that we should do well to copy this German system in our primary schools ; but for my part I would much prefer to see our primary schools endeavouring to inculcate in their pupils something of the real " public school spirit."

It would be a fair exchange if we could effect it. Give our public schools something of the intellectual efficiency of our best primary schools, and in return let the public schools give our primary schools something of that spirit of good conduct and loyalty that is so characteristic of our greatest and best schools.

But with this the public schools have more or less unconsciously created in their pupils a contempt for intellectual things which has resulted in that lack of earnestness we have already noticed. To these schools may be traced the feeling that keenness in anything intellectual is *bad form*, which results in the amateurishness not only of the British officer, but of the professional man, too. Moreover, so complete is the devotion of these schools to the classical tongues, that not only are science and modern languages placed in a most subordinate position, but even the mother tongue receives but scant respect, with the unfortunate result that the vast majority of the pupils leave school utterly unable to express themselves even in the simplest of English. Moreover, the cult of athletics, admirable as it is in reason, and fruitful as it is in minimising many of the evils of the public school system, has too often become a fetish, degrading its devotees and lowering their ideals to those of a Roman gladiator or a Greek wrestler.

Below these schools come a vast variety of so-called secondary schools equalled in their diversity only by their variations of efficiency. The vast majority of these schools are so-called private schools, subject to no public control or test whatsoever. I cannot go into a detailed description of all these English secondary schools here; suffice it to say that they are badly distributed, generally but meagrely equipped, especially for scientific instruction, the teachers, as a rule, untrained and poorly paid, the curriculum but rarely based upon any philosophical principles; in fact a hotch-potch of subjects placed in juxtaposition not upon any pedagogic principle, but in order to satisfy as many outside authorities (*i.e.*, examiners) as possible; whilst of the private schools as a whole, and, excepting a small percentage that is undoubtedly made up of exceedingly efficient schools, it can only be said that many of them are in no sense secondary; of others it would be a compliment to say that their curriculum was classical and their model the public school. The headmaster is sometimes an old elementary school teacher, at other times his qualifications are best known to himself. However, by the use of various mystic symbols duly inscribed on brass plates, and by dint of dubbing his establishment a *commercial college* or a *modern school*, he succeeds in securing victims from that large class of people who want something better and more " classy " than the public primary school supplies, but who have neither faith in nor can they afford the cost of a public school or grammar school education.

Between the comprehensive and, on the whole, fairly efficient system of primary education in England, and the non-comprehensive, varied, and perhaps, on the whole, mainly inefficient and antiquated system of secondary education in England there is to-day no co-ordination or relation; which, perhaps, is fortunate, as we may now proceed to attack the problem with our eyes open, and, let us hope, with our hearts steeled to high resolves. For in this matter we must needs be strong to be kind, and there can be no doubt but that compromise is impossible with many of the so-called private adventure schools. They must be compelled to become efficient or disappear. Efficient private schools are undoubtedly invaluable in any national system, but no self-respecting people can tolerate inefficient schools whether public or private.

Far too long, indeed, have the English school and the English child been the victims of weak compromises, and it is now time that the strong arm should cut fearlessly and effectually, for already our commercial rivals are pressing close upon us, and to make our position unassailable we must no longer tolerate inefficiency, even under the cloak of liberty.

In America alone is the democratic ideal in education to be seen in practice to-day ; and there, too, not only are its virtues, but its defects, conspicuous, by reason of their magnitude.

Practically every child between the ages of six and fourteen is found in the common schools, while for those who have shown the possession of sufficient ability there are the free high schools up to the age of eighteen, and in many States there is also a national University, free to all.

Here we have the national schools commencing in the free Kinder-Garten and culminating in the free University. Everyone with sufficient ability is welcome to take what he may from this great national store of culture. Scholarships and bursaries are not tolerated, and the system of competitive examinations for children is not allowed. The great treasure house of national culture is open to everyone who can produce the one credential, namely, desire and power to avail himself of the opportunities there offered. The passage between one department and another, between one school and the other—in a word, the *educational ladder*—is as complete and as easy as it is possible to make it. There is, first of all, the Kinder-Garten for children under six years of age, and a better Kinder-Garten than the American it would be impossible to find. Between the ages of six and fourteen the child passes through the common and grammar schools, which together are the equivalent of the European primary school. For the vast majority of American citizens this age, fourteen, marks the limit of their school life, but there are still some half million children who will proceeed to the modern secondary training, provided by the American high schools.

There is no official distinction made between these various

departments (Kinder-Garten, primary, and secondary) of the National school. All are classified under the one title of "Common Schools," and it is impossible to determine accurately what proportion of the national expenditure goes towards each of these three schools. In Europe the line of demarcation is so sharp as to be almost impassable, in America it is so faint as to be unrecognisable. And so with the teachers—no official distinctions are drawn between one class and another, and the same qualifications are required of all; all are "common school teachers." The solidarity of the teaching profession, from the humblest Kinder-Gartner ' to the High School principal, is completely admitted. There is none of that class jealousy so rampant in most European countries. England is the half-way house; in theory, at any rate, we all recognise this solidarity of the profession, in practice we make mental reservations.

We must not, however, suppose that this American democratic system of equality of opportunity is universal; on the contrary, even in America, peopled as it is largely by Europeans, there are to be found many to whom this levelling of classes in the school is most offensive. Consequently there are a considerable number of private schools which are intended to meet the needs of this exclusive class, and where the democratic ideal is conspicuous by its absence; but such schools, numerous though they be, are in no sense popular or national.

Further than this perfect co-ordination between the various parts of the American national school, must be noticed the endeavour made to foster the growth of individuality in the school. Both in the primary and in the high school, whether by means of specially selected subjects and methods, or by offering the child a large choice of subjects for study, a vigorous effort is made to nourish individuality. The military discipline and routine organisation of the best European schools are conspicuous by their absence in the American school; and, instead of the pupil being taught to rely upon his teacher for everything and upon himself for nothing, the precisely opposite course is adopted, and everything is done to foster self-resource on the part of the pupil himself. American teachers have recognised that a little power is more valuable than much knowledge.

Moreover, there is no constant appeal to authority everything is challenged to justify itself. Consequently we find that natural science and handwork occupy conspicuous and important places in the curriculum of this school.

There is this to be said for this democratic system of America—at any rate, it is alive.

Despite the fact that many of the teachers are untrained, and, indeed, but poorly educated, and that the schools are made the victims of political trickery, so powerful is this injection of the essence of democracy that the whole is seething with life and movement, and is instinct with infinite possibilities for good.

Instead of the uniformity, the practical effectiveness, the scientific adaptation of means to end, the economy, the lack of friction, and the perfect harmony of the European system, there is here an immense variety, a waste of effort, an extravagance of endeavour, a continual overlapping (for here there are no lines of demarcation between the areas of the primary and secondary school ; and, consequently, in America one hears but little of the jealous cries of " Stand off, this is our ground ! "), which, at first sight, seem to offer but poor compensation for the practical efficiency of the European system—even though the latter be bought by the sacrifice of individuality and liberty. Yet that the former offers no compensation for the sacrifice demanded I am convinced. Better the intellectual levity of America than the cultured servitude of Europe : losing liberty, what profiteth intellectuality ?

And let it not be forgotten that these aspects of democratic endeavour — superficiality, lack of effectiveness, wastefulness—are but passing phases.

Anon will the real fruit appear, when the whole people will have been educated to the standard required of true, perfect democracy, and then, as the mists and clouds rise and melt away before the rising sun, so will disappear all these blemishes, that, arising from an imperfect education, make the work of democracy so difficult to-day. Modern democracy falls away from the ideal, not because its ideal is too high, but because its training is too low. It is ignorance alone that can foul the nest of democracy; hence the eternal prayer of the true democrat is " Educate— Educate—for to educate is to live ! "

CHAPTER IV.

Difficulties.

ALREADY, in a general way, and somewhat incidentally, I have noticed some of the main difficulties that confront the effort to realize the democratic ideal in education. The greatest, and perhaps the most difficult of all, is the social obstacle arising from class distinctions and the feeling of caste that, however carefully hidden, is still the most potent of social forces. It is sometimes urged that the social problems of modern society have no place in a discussion dealing with education, but to this it must be objected that, even if one could, it is impossible to separate them. One cannot discuss or evaluate a national system of education without considering its political aspect, and it is impossible to determine its value to the State as a political machine unless one takes into account every social force that affects its efficiency. The fact is, as I have already pointed out, it is impossible to separate the national system of schools from the many other social forces that go to make up the national life.

This feeling of caste is perhaps most pronounced in Germany. Probably there is no more exclusive caste in the world than the Prussian nobles. In Germany consequently the common school is impossible, and the educational ladder a dream. In Prussia, for example, there is the *Volksschulen* for the labouring classes, the Real schools for the mercantile and commercial classes, and the Gymnasien or classical schools for the professional, official, and higher classes of society.   As a rule, a boy enters one of these three schools at six years of age and remains there until the completion of his school life.   When he leaves he proceeds to fill one of the particular posts in the national machine that his school life has fitted him for, and no other.   In some towns where democratic ideas are growing, boys sometimes attend the Volksschulen until they are nine and then proceed to the particular secondary school where they will receive their special training for life; but this is unusual.   Generally speaking, as I have said, the caste feeling is so strong that it is as impossible for a German boy to pass from one school to another as it is for his father to rise from one class of society to another.

Although France has no great landlord class corresponding to the Prussian nobles or the English squirearchy and aristocracy, and despite the existence of a republic built upon the watchwords of " Liberty, Equality, and Fraternity," yet in but few countries are the distinctions of class more closely observed or more rigidly enforced.   The gulf between the workman and *bourgeoisie* is only equalled in depth and impassibility by that between the latter and the highest classes.   There is nothing more repugnant to the French mind—especially the maternal mind—than the *promiscuité* that would be the consequence of the democratic common school.   Consequently such a school is unknown in France, and we have instead special schools for special classes of society.   The primary schools of France are of two kinds: the secular State school, in which about two-thirds of all the primary scholars are found, and the religious Church schools, which are educating about one-third of the children.

The well-to-do middle and upper classes do not send their children to these schools, but at from six to nine years of age they are incarcerated in the secondary schools either as full boarders or as day boarders.   Here again there is practically no common school and no educational ladder.

In England, although democratic ideas are gradually permeating the mass of society from below upwards, yet so strong is this caste feeling, and so acute in some respects are the class distinctions of society, that despite the fact that there is in this country but one comprehensive system of State schools, certain classes, more particularly the lower middle classes, persist in sending their children to schools which, generally speaking, offer no guarantee of efficiency, and indeed cannot under existing conditions provide an adequate and satisfactory system of training for their pupils. The upper middle classes and the highest classes of English society have at their disposal schools where a certain well known and specific system of training can be obtained; but even in these schools the instruction given is of a singularly antiquated character, and in many respects unfitted for the strenuous life of to-day.

But between these two systems—the public primary system and the public school system—there is a great gap, filled in a very haphazard fashion by private schools, for which, as a class, no one has yet found a good word to say. So that in England, between this petty feeling of caste and the absence of an efficient system of cheap day second grade schools the lower middle classes are growing up destitute of any real education. This is a great national loss, for among this great class much of the intellectual capital of the nation is stored. As a class they are frugal, moderate and thrifty, and they are recruited from the best of the lower classes; consequently they are storing up from year to year sound minds in healthy bodies; and I am sure that, were an efficient system of training provided for them by the State, there would soon appear an immense increase in the intellectual capital of the community.

Besides this social difficulty there is the very serious religious difficulty, to which I have elsewhere referred. In Germany primary scholars are segregated in schools entirely according to sect. Each school is denominational, being either Lutheran, Catholic, or Jewish. Although it sometimes happens, as at Crefeld, Cologne, etc., that one finds Lutheran and Catholic schools under one roof, yet each is absolutely independent and distinct, having its own text books, its own teachers, and its own managers and inspectors (local). This system is perhaps tolerable in Germany, because the great Lutheran and Catholic churches constitute the vast bulk of the people, but it undoubtedly constitutes a most serious hardship to the Free or Reformed churchmen, as well as to atheists, etc., whilst to the powerful social democratic party it is offensive; for so long as this system of separate sectarian schools persists, the democratic common school is impossible. The struggle between Church and State in Germany is of long standing, and, though at one time it appeared certain to result in the complete supremacy of the State, yet recent events have shown that the Church as a political force is still one of the most potent in Prussia, and that she is still able to wring concessions from the official bureaucracy representing the State. For example, the *local* clerical inspector, though controlling the school, has hitherto acted as official subordinate to the Government inspector. This subordination will in future be replaced by co-ordination, and the *local* inspector will, to all intents and purposes, act as the official equal of the Government inspector. Thus the fate of the school and the teacher will, more than ever, be at the mercy of these representatives of the Church, who, it must be remembered, have had no practical training for the work, except what they may have acquired by a few weeks' course in a training college before they received their appointment as cleric.

A similar condition of things prevails, to a very large extent, in the Prussian secondary school also. Here, again, the schools are classified according as they are Lutheran, Catholic, or Jewish; but, of course, such a division is only possible in the larger and wealthier centres of population: the smaller and poorer districts must content themselves with some modification of this plan; and, consequently, in such places we find the children of the various sects attending the one school and receiving the secular instruction in common, whilst for the religious instruction they are separated into sects. In such cases the sectarian teaching is given either by one of the ordinary teachers or, if the number of pupils of one sect be small, and the school has no teacher belonging to that sect, the local cleric belonging to that sect may come in and give the children the necessary instruction.

This separation of the children in the school according to sects, and also the existence of separate sectarian schools, are deplored by many of the best German teachers. It is felt that this perpetuating in the school of sectarian differences and jealousies is most unfortunate; and the fact that separate text-books have to be provided for these different schools is very significant, and emphasises the pernicious effects of recognising in the State schools those differences which in the past have cost Germany so much, but which, in the future, it is hoped, may disappear. This disappearance, however, can only be effected by adopting a different policy in the national schools.

The question is being asked, indeed, even as it is in many other countries, whether it is only by exclusion of all religion from the school that unity can be attained. It is sad to think that the foundation rock upon which national, like individual, character is mainly built must be severely ignored in school work if peace is to be attained. In France this momentous step has been taken, and all the State schools, primary and secondary, are purely secular. In place of religious instruction the curriculum of the French primary school provides a course in moral instruction; but either the indifference of the teachers or the invertebrate character of the material has produced results which are admittedly disappointing, and, in many respects, unfortunate. Indeed, any form of ethical training, whether it be termed " moral " or " religious," depends for its success entirely upon the personality of the teacher, and any course of instruction which by its own rationalism tends to modify rather than heighten the enthusiasm of the teacher will have but slight effect on the character of the pupils. The course is admirable, but not for children. One must appeal to the heart, not to the head of the child, and to the head, and not to the heart, of the man. Frenchmen are too logical. Admitting the equality of the sexes, they have proceeded to treat them as identical, and the French high schools for girls are close copies of those for boys, and again in this matter of moral instruction the same defect is observable; they treat child and man as identical.

E 2

In the State secondary schools outside pastors may attend, if required, and give religious instruction in the school to those requesting it.

However, this secularisation of the State school has not solved the religious difficulty in France—indeed, it has increased it. As I have already stated, one-third of all French primary scholars are to-day (or were before the recent action against the Congregations) being taught in private Church schools, supported entirely by the poor Catholics of France to the extent of about two and a-quarter million pounds annually, while in the realm of secondary education the Church schools are annually growing at the expense of the State schools to such an extent as to seriously alarm the French Government; and this growth has, it is asserted, led to the recent crusade against these private primary and secondary schools.

In America, too, the State schools are secular, and here the same results have appeared as in France, but on a smaller scale. The Lutheran immigrants from Scandinavia and Germany, as well as the great community of Catholics—which latter numbers over twelve million people—refuse to utilise the State secular schools, and so has arisen the system of so-called parochial schools in America, in which between one and two million children are being annually educated.*

The growth of these schools, particularly of the Lutheran schools, however, is not altogether due to the religious question, but arises largely from the fact that English alone may be used as the medium of instruction in all American schools.

Americans feel that their one hope of consolidating the cosmopolitan crowd of immigrants, and converting them as rapidly as possible into American citizens, is through the work of the school, and that for this purpose no

---

* It is interesting to observe that the "religious difficulty," of which so much is heard in England and France, excites but slight public attention in Germany where the Church is so strong, or in America where it is so weak. It is only where the forces are nearly balanced that the battle becomes so bitter.

language but English must be tolerated in the school; but to this the German objects, and so he provides himself with a school where German may be utilised and taught. However, at home the German himself is pursuing the American policy, and, despite the fact that nearly three-quarters of a million children in Prussia cannot speak German, he relentlessly insists on German alone being used whether it be in German Poland, Schleswig-Holstein or Alsace-Lorraine. So, too, does the great French Republic treat its three million Breton citizens, whose home tongue is not French. In England wiser counsels have prevailed.

Besides these social and political difficulties, there are pedagogic difficulties in the way of carrying out the democratic ideal; but these are transitory and only call for further investigation. It will be well, however, to refer very briefly to some of them here. These difficulties arise largely from attempting to graft the ideals of democracy on to the present curricula rather than commencing *de novo*.

Thus the present primary school curriculum has no direct relationship with the secondary school curriculum. The basis of the primary school course is the mother tongue, of the secondary school course the classical tongues; and though, as we have argued, the study of the mother tongue of the primary scholar should lead up to the study of other tongues by the secondary scholar, yet under present conditions this foundation of knowledge of the mother tongue which the pupil possesses is neither developed nor fostered in any way in the secondary school: on the contrary, it is often deliberately snubbed and neglected. Instead of building upon the mother tongue, the secondary school adopts a system and methods of teaching as alien as possible to the spirit of the home tongue and as repulsive as possible to the inquiring and acquisitive spirit of a vigorous childhood. And more, so aggressive is this tyranny of classicism that it has actually succeeded in foisting its own ghoulish garments on the bright spirit of the living tongue, and the primary scholar becomes, through his *grammar* studies, but another victim on the altar of classicism. Hence the pupil who has completed the primary school course finds his training quite unsuitable for the work of the secondary school. The one does not lead up to the other; consequently, in both America and Wales, where an attempt is being made to carry out our ideal, it is found that the primary school pupil comes up to the secondary school with but a poor preparation for the work.

An attempt is made to meet the difficulty by providing special preparation for the secondary studies in the primary school either by grafting on secondary studies to the primary curriculum or by forming special classes for these pupils. Both plans are objectionable in theory, and most unsatisfactory in practice. The smattering of secondary studies provided by the first plan is more than useless, it is pernicious, to those who do not proceed to the secondary school; while the second plan differentiates where all should be equal. Until the secondary school is prepared to take the trained product of the primary school as its basis upon which to build, this difficulty will be felt.

The independence of the primary school must be acknowledged; but, unfortunately for our schoolmasters, this step will involve the overthrow of the supremacy of the classics in the secondary school. These will have to be content with a position subordinate to that of the mother tongue, but equal to that of modern tongues. Admitting, however, that this step be taken, and that the primary scholar proceeds at the age of fourteen to commence his secondary studies, as is the rule in America, is not this age too late, and is not the time left for secondary school studies—namely, four years— much too short for any really thorough secondary training? It is difficult to answer these questions in the light of our experience, but it is undoubtedly the opinion of many experts that secondary studies, particularly linguistic studies, are generally begun too early, and that a more intensive study at a later age (say, twelve or fourteen) will be found much more effective in the end.

Personally, I am convinced that we begin all our studies, primary and secondary, much too early. We are in far too great a hurry to make men and women of our boys and girls. However that may be, no definite answers can be given to the questions just put ; for until the principles of solidarity of curricula and the mutual independence of schools are admitted it is impossible to say that the age of beginning is too late or the period of training too short.

Finally, there is the difficulty of selecting the children who shall receive à secondary education, for it is obvious that the community cannot be burdened with the task of endeavouring to put a " two-thousand-dollar education into a five-cent boy." One thing is certain—no system of competitive examinations can do this. If there is one phase of English education that is more ludicrously pathetic than another it is this extraordinary system of competitive examinations of children, by which we endeavour to sift out the ore from the matrix. It is recognised by most cultured Englishmen that it is the development of a strong individuality in the citizens that has contributed to the success of the Saxon. Yet here we have a system deliberately contrived to crush out all variety of personality in our children. It is bad enough for young people to be subjected to such a system ; it is wanton waste to put children to such tests. No, the only person who by constant observation can determine the capacity of children is the teacher, and it is to the teacher we must look for relief from this system of competitive examinations. The solidarity of the profession which will result from the application of democratic ideals to education will bring about a closer union and a better understanding between our primary and secondary teachers. It will be recognised that both are engaged in precisely the same task, and that perfect co-operation is indispensable for the success of that task. Consequently a committee composed of both primary and secondary teachers will be recognised as a far more effective machine for discovering the intellectual jewels of the people than the present system, of which it may be said that no other could be worse and any other must be better.

So much for the difficulties of democracy. None of them is fatal, and the solution of all is—*education !*

But let us not forget that it is not so much more education as a better education that is needed,

CHAPTER V.

Conclusions.

WE have already noticed some of the difficulties that confront the work of democracy in the field of education, and we concluded that all the social difficulties and most of the administrative difficulties will disappear as the results of a better system of popular education appear. The fact that the school has sometimes been made the victim of political jobbery only emphasises the necessity of securing to each citizen an intelligent appreciation of the principles of politics and economics. The essentials of political ecoonmy should, I hold, be taught in every school. Jobbery fattens on ignorance and thrives on prejudice. Eternal vigilance, it has been said, is the price of liberty, and to be vigilant a people must be intelligent. And so for the prejudices of class and the rivalries of sectarianism education and national culture alone are panaceas of whose efficacy there can be no doubt.

Of the difficulties arising from the poverty of rural communities, of those arising from variations in social conditions outside the school, it is unnecessary to speak here. Suffice it to say that all these difficulties are common in a greater or less degree to every great civilised community. The growth of world-citizenship and the gradual disappearance of national characteristics are two of the most significant of modern movements; while the fact already noted, that beneath the apparent variety and diversity on the surface of the life of modern communities there is a remarkable similarity in the deeper currents that agitate and stimulate the peoples, is of immense significance.

It is the recognition of this truth, that although no nation can be a pattern, yet it may always be a guide to another nation, that makes the comparative study of modern systems of national education so valuable. The experience of Germany, of America, and of France to England is invaluable; but that experience must be read through our own eyes.

Let us glance for a moment at certain aspects of our educational system as it appears in the light of foreign experience.

In England nearly eighteen per cent. of the total population are found in the public primary schools; in Germany, as a whole, there are also eighteen per cent. of the people in the State primary schools; in France, where the children are fewer in proportion to the total population, the proportion in the schools (*i.e.*, State and Church schools) is about sixteen per cent.; while in America in all kinds of schools, primary and secondary, there are to be found one-fifth of the total population.

In Germany there are many overcrowded class-rooms, under-staffed schools, and half-day schools; but the teacher is in all respects the best trained and most skilful of pedagogues. In France there are some overcrowded schools, and many untrained teachers. In England there are many untrained teachers and poor school buildings; while in America the average rural teacher is wretchedly paid, and professionally unequipped, and the school is often poorly housed. Generally speaking, one may summarise the matter by saying that, in most respects, there is no essential difference between the *schools* of these four countries, but that of the *teachers* there are in all four countries but two classes—those professionally equipped and those not so equipped—and that of those professionally prepared Germany possesses the greatest proportion and America the least.

When, however, we come to the field of so-called secondary education, England's lamentable lack is at once apparent. In America it is estimated that practically one per cent. of the nation are receiving a higher education; thus in the year 1899-1900 the number of American secondary students is given as 719,241, in France in 1897 the number of boys attending public and private secondary schools was 182,221, while some 12,000 girls were found in the public secondary schools for girls. Of the girls who attend the private conventual schools the number is not known, but is, doubtless, very large. In Prussia, in 1898-9, the total number of boys attending secondary schools was 152,019, while of girls there are over 150,000 in higher schools. In England, in 1897, the number of boys who were returned as receiving some kind of secondary education was 158,502, and of girls 133,042; but it must be emphasised that but a fraction of these are receiving an education that is in any respect comparable to the education received by the French or German secondary scholar. This is indeed the most pressing problem in English education to-day—the provision of day secondary schools open to all.

There is, however, no need as yet to despair of English education. In the primary school we need more trained teachers, and those better trained; we need to place our rural schools on an equality with our town schools. Money must be spent on building new schools and improving old ones. In the secondary schools we need trained professional teachers possessing security of tenure and reasonable rewards; we need to modernise our curricula and to rationalise our methods; and, finally, we need co-ordination between these schools, so that the gifted pupil may pass easily from primary to secondary school. But, in attacking these problems, our success will depend upon the ideals that animate us, for we work not alone for ourselves, nor our children, but for our children's children; and, although you and I cannot hope to see the fruition of our endeavours, yet let us sow the good seed of democracy, trusting that in due season will appear a plant pointing heavenwards and worthy to look upon. We, who are at last about to set up a national system of education, primary and secondary, will work with no mean aim of immediate profit or commercial success ; we will lay our foundation firm and lasting as the everlasting hills. The common good shall be our aim, not of to-day nor of to-morrow only, but also of the many morrows yet to come. For fair must be the stone, true must be its place, and firm the hand of the builder if the foundation is to be well and truly laid upon which the great edifice of true democracy is to be reared. There must be no chipping of the stone to fit the place : rather must the place be made to fit the stone. We can tolerate no compromise that may spoil the symmetry and ultimately wreck the effectiveness of the whole. Upon the system of education that we to-day build, and, in the end, upon the ideals that animate us in the building will depend the character of English democracy to-morrow. Let us then build with infinite patience this temple of national culture, let us see to it that its pinnacles and spires point true to the stars, and that its foundations are laid deep and firm upon the solid rock of national character.

We can build such a temple only by mutual co-operation and sacrifice, for the true life is a constant sacrifice, and he who best serves himself serves the State. Patriotism is the best selfishness, and he who loses himself in the people finds himself in the State. To work for self is to work for all, for the happiness of all is dependent on the happiness of one. No community is efficient that has one inefficient.

Wealth can be created, it cannot be acquired. A father may under present conditions leave his son a certain number of metal coins, but he cannot leave him a grain of that mental power which he himself possesses, and which alone is of any real and permanent value.

And this temple of national culture of which we have spoken is well worthy of our most strenuous efforts and deepest thoughts, for not only will the beauty and symmetry of the whole be a criterion of our ideal, but upon it and within it will be hung all those emblems of the national life that have most deeply appealed to our people ; there they will hang as mementos of the past and beacons of the future. Moreover, in this temple will be stored all the intellectual capital of the people, and to it every child will come freely and gladly to partake of whatever portion of that capital is his. Between him and it none shall stand. God himself shall be the arbiter, for He alone can award the proper and peculiar portion of each.

And having obtained his share he will go out into life to do with his talents as seemeth best, and in due time will he return his talents ten-fold, nay, a hundred-fold, to the common stock in the temple. There in this temple is stored the only real national capital.

The stability and permanency of the State is dependent not upon its annual surplus, but upon the number of cultured healthy citizens the schools are turning out.

Just as the rising sun scatters the mist, so will a better and broader culture chase away the mammon of unrighteousness and the greed of commerce that to-day enthral our people.

It is sad to think that to obtain progress in education appeal must be made to the commercial instinct and greed of the English people. At present education, for its own sake, does not appeal to them, so one must needs alarm them with bogeys of American and German competition. It was not thus with Germany. Hurled to the dust by a ruthless conqueror, she determined to make herself once more worthy of freedom and glory by training, by education. She recognised that it is righteousness alone that can exalt a people, and so, leaving to France the empire of the land, and to England that of the sea, she was content to attain to the empire of the intellect, knowing that in God's good time even those other things may be added to her domain. However, even in England progress is being made: the cry of the politician and the sectarian is daily becoming feebler, and their power for evil is being lessened. There is a growing feeling that it is time that the nation's school should be what its name implies.

Moreover, as the power of the people is more and more

felt, so its effect is being seen in the schools. The people themselves — particularly the great progressive cities of England — are crying out for equal opportunity and good schools for all. Trades union congresses discuss this question of national education, and are • asking for better schools and free schools, primary and secondary, and wherever workmen are well organised and themselves educated, there one finds an efficient system of education.*

It is in rural England, where the dead hand lies heavy on the land, that the school is poorest and weakest, and only as the leaven of a better public opinion slowly penetrates into these spots will matters improve.

Finally, in a better education alone is our salvation, not because we may possibly thereby have larger surpluses, but because we shall certainly have more good citizens ; and these good citizens, let it not be forgotten, must be cultured, it is true, but they must also be healthy. Hence the futility of an educational reform that is not preceded by certain social reforms. We must aim at building up complete men, men who are not only good scholars but good animals also, and this we cannot hope to do while so many of our people are housed under conditions intolerable to animals, and fatal to manhood.

This movement towards democracy, though repugnant to many, cannot be stayed. Slow, almost imperceptible, is the movement at times, yet anon there is a perfect cataract of motion. It is the part of the wise man to recognise it, and, as far as possible, control it, so that the intermittent may be replaced by a permanent movement, and the destructiveness of the cataract be avoided. To guide such

---

* " The public attitude controls, and will always control, to a certain extent, the work of the school ; and only when our folk have reluctantly come to the conclusion that all Englishmen are not born educational experts may the teacher hope for freedom from the ignorant criticism that to-day so much harasses and fetters him. Public opinion in Germany is very much like public opinion in England, but there is this important distinction—the German workman believes that some men know more about education than he does, the Englishman does not."

a movement to its noble end should be the ideal of statesmanship; and though the desert be long and the difficulties many, though the cloud of fire be but faint that illumines the dark track, yet there in the distance will Pisgah anon appear, from whose heights the seer will behold the fair land beyond.

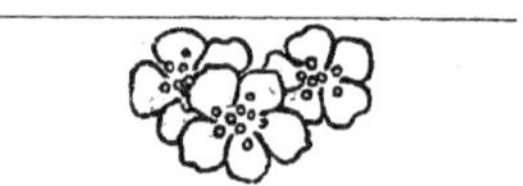